First American Edition 2016
Kane Miller, A Division of EDC Publishing

Text copyright © 2015 Sally Rippin
Illustrations copyright © Alisa Coburn 2015
Logo and design copyright © Hardie Grant Egmont 2015

First published in Australia in 2015 by Hardie Grant Egmont

For information contact:
Kane Miller, A Division of EDC Publishing
P.O. Box 470663
Tulsa, OK 74147-0663

www.kanemiller.com
www.edcpub.com
www.usbornebooksandmore.com

Library of Congress Control Number: 2015938841

Printed and bound in China
2 3 4 5 6 7 8 9 10

ISBN: 978-1-61067-456-0

Billie's UNDERWATER ADVENTURE

by Sally Rippin

illustrated by Alisa Coburn

Kane Miller
A DIVISION OF EDC PUBLISHING

Billie B. Brown STOMPS into preschool.

STOMP!
STOMP!
STOMP!

She doesn't want
to be there today.

But then Billie peeks into the classroom.
Something very interesting is going on.

POP!

Can you guess what it is?

"Come over here, Billie,"
says Miss Amy. "We're going
on an underwater adventure."

POP!

"Who wants to be a mermaid?" asks Miss Amy.

Me! calls Zara.

Me! says Billie.

But Billie is too slow.

"We only have one mermaid tail," says Miss Amy.
"You can be an octopus, Billie."

Billie frowns.

"I'll be an octopus!"
shouts Billie's friend Jack.

"I want to be a mermaid,"
Billie grumbles. "I want a tail."

"But I asked first!" says Zara.

Billie crosses her arms and
sticks out her bottom lip.

I don't want
to play then,
she mutters.

"You can have a turn after Zara," Miss Amy tells Billie. "Or how about I make you into …

… a great glittery sea creature?"

Billie looks down at her costume.

She feels a smile wriggle across her face.

"And here is the great blue sea!"
says Miss Amy. "Off you go! But
be back in time for fruit snack!"

Billie, Zara and Jack dive
into the foamy waves.

They swim down

deep

deep

deep into the water.

All around them
little silver, pink and gold fish
flit and spin.

"Over here!" calls Billie.
"This way to the castle!"

Billie leads her friends
through tall wavy seaweed.

Don't get
tangled!
yells Billie.

Next, they swim over
a sparkling coral reef.

Don't get
scratched!
calls Jack.

Don't get
lost,
yells Zara.

Last of all, they fight their way
through a huge school of fish.

LOOK!
shouts Billie.

"There's the castle!
It's not far now!"

When Billie, Jack and Zara
swim into the castle, they
find a long table laid with
a delicious sea banquet.

They munch on seashell
cakes, starfish pies and
seaweed spaghetti.

When they are thirsty,
they sip on anemone tea.

Suddenly, there is a ROAR! at the window.

A great gloopy sea monster sticks its big gooby head in.

"Who's that eating my morning snack?" it growls.

Billie quickly pulls her friends underneath the table.

Oh no! The great grumbling, growling sea monster is squeezing through the window. What can they do?

I'm scared! whispers Jack.

Me too, squeaks Zara.

Just then, Billie has an idea.

A **Super-duper** idea.

She unties the long sparkly
material from around her.

Then bravely she scrambles
out from under the table.

Billie throws the sparkly material over the monster.

It howls and writhes and thrashes, but the more it twists and turns, the tighter it is caught.

"Quick! Let's get away!" says Jack.

"But, Billie, how will you swim
without your tail?" asks Zara.

"Don't worry,"
says Billie. "If you
hold my hand
I'll be okay."

Together, Billie and
   her friends swim through
      the sun-sparkling water …

up

up

up

… and burst up
  out of the waves.

Just in time
for fruit snack.